VIKING

The Story of a Raider

Dee Phillips

READZONE

READZONE

First published in this edition 2014

The right of the Author to be identified as the Author of this work has been asserted by the Author in accordance with the Copyright, Designs and Patents Act 1988

Every attempt has been made by the Publisher to secure appropriate permissions for material reproduced in this book. If there has been any oversight we will be happy to rectify the situation in future editions or reprints. Written submissions should be made to the Publishers.

British Library Cataloguing in Publication Data (CIP) is available for this title.

ISBN 978-1-78322-517-0

Printed in Malta by Melita Press

Developed and Created by Ruby Tuesday Books Ltd
Project Director – Ruth Owen
Designer – Elaine Wilkinson

Images courtesy of Alamy (page 34bl), Shutterstock and Superstock (page 17b, 25b).

Acknowledgements
With thanks to Lorraine Petersen, Educational Consultant, for her help in the development and creation of these books

Visit our website: www.readzonebooks.com

It was my first raid.

My sword slashed through flesh.

My axe hacked through bone.

Now I was a Viking warrior.

VIKING

The Story of a Raider

They came from the wild, icy
north of Europe.
Their ships were sleek and fast.
They came in search of wealth and slaves.
In the 800s, people in Britain, Ireland
and other parts of Europe lived in fear.

The raiders from the north could
attack at any time.
The attackers showed no mercy.
They had no fear.

They were…

the Vikings.

I wait in the early
morning darkness.
The icy waves slap the
side of the ship.
My heart beats fast, but
I am not afraid.
Viking blood runs through
my veins.

If I die today, I will die a

Viking warrior.

We wait in the early
morning darkness.
Soon the sun will rise.
Then we will attack.

My heart beats fast, but
I am not afraid.

To die a Viking warrior is
a good death.

A memory fills my head.
A long, dark winter night.
A fire burns.
My father tells of a bloody battle.

My nurse holds me close.
I fall asleep in her arms to a
story of great warriors.

My father is the chieftain
of our tribe.
He is strong and fearless.
He taught me to fight with
a sword and an axe.
His Viking blood runs
through my veins.

Memories fill my head.
My mother, so beautiful.
But always so sad.

Long, dark winter nights.
My nurse holding me close.
Singing to me softly.

Memories of my village fill my head.

I am watching old Erik.
A fire burns.
In the heat of the fire, glowing iron
becomes an axe.

I am watching young Horik.
In his hands, a tree becomes a dragon.
A dragon for a Viking ship.

17

I grew strong and fearless.
My father gave me a
sword and an axe.
Soon I would go to sea.

"I will be a great warrior,"
I told my nurse.
"The life of a farmer is a
good life, too," she said.

I laughed at her then.
"You are only a slave," I said.
"You have no Viking blood.
You do not understand."

When I was 18, I went to sea.
We pushed our ship out into
the icy black waves.
From the shore, the slave woman
watched me go.

By day, we rowed.
At night, we slept wrapped in seal skins.
Then the great day came.

It was my first raid.
I leapt from the ship with
my father.
I knew what I had to do.

My sword slashed through flesh.
My axe hacked through bone.

It was my first raid.
I carried gold and silver back to our ship.
We left the men of that place dying.
We dragged their women to our ship to be slaves.

I had become a

Viking warrior.

Now I have been on
many raids.

As the sun rises, we wait.
In the early morning light,
I see small stone huts.

Soon we will attack.
My heart beats fast, but I am
not afraid.

Then it is time.
My father, strong and
fearless, is beside me.

We row hard to the shore.
With a terrible yell we leap
into the water.
People run from the stone huts,
screaming.

My sword slashes through flesh.
My axe hacks through bone.
The Viking blood burns in my veins.
But something feels wrong.

I stand among the dying men.

 screams my father.

But something feels wrong.
I know this place.

I know these small stone huts.

Memories fill my head.
I am wrapped in soft wool.
A woman holds me close.
She sings to me softly.

Memories fill my head.

Men. Huge, wild men coming
from the sea.
The woman. My mother holds
me close as she runs.
But we cannot escape.

We are dragged to the ship.
Dragged to a Viking ship.

My father is before me.
He is strong and fearless.

he screams.
But the blood in my veins
has turned to ice.

"I know this place," I say.
"I am of this place."

My father, the warrior, falls to his knees.

"Tell me," I scream.

He says, "I captured a slave."

"She had a young boy. A strong, fearless boy."

"Your mother could not bear children."

"A warrior needs a son."

Memories fill my head.

My mother. The Viking.
Beautiful and sad.

My mother. The slave.
Holding me close.

My father stands before me.
"Fight, Viking," he says.
My heart beats fast.
I feel the blood running
through my veins.

The blood of a slave...

        ...or the blood of a Viking?

Vikings:

Behind the Story

The age of the Vikings lasted for more than 200 years, from around AD 800 to 1050.

The Vikings came from the area that today is made up of Norway, Sweden and Denmark. In many places the land was mountainous. It was easier to travel by river or sea than over land. So the Vikings became skilful boat builders and sailors.

The Vikings were farmers, growing crops and raising animals. Farming was a tough life in the icy, rocky north, however. So raiding parties of warriors left their villages in search of wealth. Viking raiders sailed to Britain, Ireland and other parts of Europe. They attacked coastal settlements, stealing precious goods, killing some people and capturing others as slaves. In time, Vikings even explored parts of North America.

Viking Longships

- The Vikings sailed in longships. A large ship might carry 120 warriors.
- A longship had a large, square sail woven from wool. It was also powered by the warriors rowing.
- The ship had a prow at both ends. This allowed the men to make a quick getaway from the shore without needing to turn the ship around.

The Vikings weren't only raiders, though. They were also traders. They travelled to faraway places such as Russia and Turkey. They sold animal furs and slaves, and bought silk and other luxury goods.

Map of the Viking World

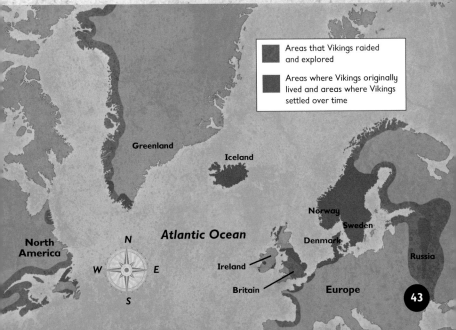

Areas that Vikings raided and explored

Areas where Vikings originally lived and areas where Vikings settled over time

Greenland

Iceland

Norway

Sweden

North America

N

Atlantic Ocean

Denmark

Russia

W   E

Ireland

Britain   Europe

S

Viking – What's next?

Look at the pictures on pages 10–11, 14–15 and 16–17. They show the young Viking's memories of his childhood. Create a collage picture that shows your most important memories.

The young warrior says, *"Viking blood runs through my veins."* Being a Viking is important to his sense of identity.

Write three short sentences that sum up who you are. Is your sense of identity to do with where you come from? Perhaps it's about the things you enjoy doing. What runs through your veins?

Everything the young Viking feels about his identity and life is tied up in being a Viking. How does he feel when he discovers he is really the son of a slave and the Vikings aren't his birth family? With a partner, role-play the conversation he has with his father.

• The young warrior has been raised a Viking. Is his upbringing more important than blood? Is his Viking father's love enough to make him feel like a true Viking?

• Will he be able to go on future raids knowing the people he attacks might be his true people?

The book's two female characters appear only briefly, but they are important. Discuss their roles in the story.

• Why do you think the young warrior's adopted Viking mother was sad?

• How did his real mother feel to be taken from her home to become a slave to her own son?

Titles in the
Yesterday's Voices
series

VIKING
The Story of a Raider
Dee Phillips

We jump from our ship and attack. But something feels wrong. I know this place....

SAMURAI
The Story of a Warrior
Dee Phillips

We face each other. Two proud samurai. Revenge burns in my heart.

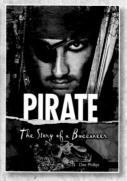

PIRATE
The Story of a Buccaneer
Dee Phillips

We saw a treasure ship. Up went our black flag. They could not escape....

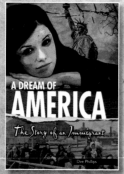

A DREAM OF AMERICA
The Story of an Immigrant
Dee Phillips

The work is so hard. I miss my home. Will my dream of America come true?

RESISTANCE FIGHTER
The Story of a Secret War
Dee Phillips

I jumped from the plane. I carried fake papers, a gun and a radio. Now I was Sylvie, a resistance fighter....

VIETNAM
The Story of a Marine
Dee Phillips

Every day we went on patrol. The Viet Cong hid in jungles and villages. We had to find them, before they found us.

x